JAGUARS
World's Strongest Cats

Amelie von Zumbusch

PowerKiDS
press

New York

Published in 2007 by The Rosen Publishing Group, Inc.
29 East 21st Street, New York, NY 10010

First Edition

Book Design: Erica Clendening
Layout Design: Julio Gil

Photo Credits: Cover, p. 1 © www.istockphoto.com/Daniel Leon; pp. 4, 8, 10, 16, 18 © www.shutterstock.com; p. 6 © www.istockphoto.com/Rachael Arnott; pp. 12, 14 © www.istockphoto.com/Jason Pacheco; p. 20 U.S. Fish and Wildlife Service. Photo by John and Karen Hollingsworth.

Library of Congress Cataloging-in-Publication Data

Zumbusch, Amelie von.
  Jaguars : world's strongest cats / Amelie von Zumbusch. — 1st ed.
      p. cm. — (Dangerous cats)
  Includes index.
  ISBN-13: 978-1-4042-3628-8 (library binding)
  ISBN-10: 1-4042-3628-7 (library binding)
  1. Jaguar—Juvenile literature. I. Title.
  QL737.C23Z795 2007
  599.75'5—dc22
                                                2006019527

Manufactured in the United States of America

Contents

The Jaguar

The jaguar is a strong, **fierce** member of the cat family. The jaguar is one of the four animals that **scientists** list as great cats. The great cats are the largest kinds of cats. The jaguar is the only great cat that lives in North America and South America.

The Native Americans of South America call the jaguar the *yaguara*. This means "the animal that kills in one **leap**." The English word "jaguar" comes from *yaguara*.

Jaguars are smaller than lions and tigers. However, they are larger than leopards.

Where Jaguars Live

Jaguars live in South America, Central America, and the southern parts of North America. Jaguars used to live throughout the southwestern United States. However there are few or no wild jaguars living in the United States today.

Jaguars live in a number of different **habitats**. Many jaguars live in the **rain forest**. Other jaguars live in grasslands or woods. Jaguars always live near water. They are one of the few cats that like to swim.

Jaguars are one of the many animals that live in rain forests. More than half of the animals in the world live in rain forests.

A Spotted Cat

Most jaguars have a yellow or orange coat with black markings on it. Jaguars have black spots on their head and legs. They have black **rosettes** on their back.

Jaguars look much like leopards. There are several ways to tell the two great cats apart. For example, jaguars are larger. They have more powerful bodies than do leopards. Jaguars also have spots inside of some of their rosettes. Leopards have no spots in their rosettes.

Every jaguar has a different set of markings on its face.

Black Panthers

Some jaguars are totally black. Black jaguars also have spots. However, you can see these spots only when a black jaguar stands in the bright sunlight.

Black jaguars often live deep in the rain forest. It is very dark there. Their dark coats make these jaguars hard to see.

Black jaguars are sometimes called black panthers. Some leopards also have black spots on a black background. They are called black panthers, too.

Can you see the spots on this black jaguar?

Jaguar Cubs

Baby jaguars are called cubs. Mother jaguars hide their cubs in a den. This keeps the cubs safe from **predators**.

A mother jaguar has between one and four cubs at a time. When the cubs are first born, they cannot walk. They weigh between 25 and 29 ounces (.7–.8 kg). The cubs drink their mother's milk. In time they grow strong enough to walk and play.

When jaguar cubs are born, they cannot see. They do not open their eyes until they are about two weeks old.

Growing Up

Jaguar cubs play and **wrestle** together, as all baby cats do. This helps them gain skills they will need later in life. They also learn skills by watching their mother.

The cubs live with their mother until they are about two years old. The young jaguars then go off to live on their own. Except for mothers and their cubs, jaguars spend most of their time alone. Each jaguar lives in its own **territory**.

These jaguar cubs are practicing important skills when they play with each other.

Meat Eaters

Jaguars are predators. They eat many different kinds of animals. Sometimes they eat large animals, such as deer. At other times they eat smaller animals, such as mice and turtles. They even eat fish, birds, and monkeys.

Jaguars have sharp teeth and a strong mouth. A jaguar's mouth is so strong that it can bite through a turtle's shell. Jaguars often kill their **prey** by biting through the bones of its head.

Jaguars are the top predator in their habitat. This means that no other animal will hunt a full-grown jaguar.

18

Jaguars creep up on their prey. When it is very close, a jaguar leaps on its prey and kills it. Jaguars most often hunt on the ground. They sometimes climb trees to hunt. When its prey walks by, a jaguar jumps down from the tree.

These great cats are also good at fishing. Jaguars wait quietly next to a river or stream. When a fish swims by, the jaguar catches the fish in its sharp claws.

Jaguars keep a close watch on their prey as they creep toward it.

20

A Fierce Cat

Jaguars **avoid** people much of the time. They do not often hurt people. Native Americans in South America even tell stories about jaguars that came out of the Amazon rain forest to play with children.

However, jaguars are fierce, strong cats. People should always be very careful around jaguars. If a person makes a jaguar afraid, the cat might charge at that person. The jaguar's sharp claws and teeth can be very **dangerous**.

For its size, the jaguar is the strongest of all the cats.

Jaguars and People

Jaguars sometimes kill farm animals, such as cows, for food. Farmers often kill these jaguars to stop them from eating more farm animals. Other people hunt jaguars for their fur. This is because some people like to wear clothes made from this great cat's beautiful coat.

When people take over land to build farms, houses, and businesses, some jaguars lose their territories. Luckily some people have formed parks where jaguars can live safely.

Glossary

avoid (uh-VOYD) To stay away from something.

dangerous (DAYN-jeh-rus) Might cause hurt.

fierce (FEERS) Strong and ready to fight.

habitats (HA-beh-tatz) The kinds of land where an animal or a plant naturally lives.

leap (LEEP) A jump.

predators (PREH-duh-terz) Animals that kill other animals for food.

prey (PRAY) Animals that are hunted by another animal for food.

rain forest (RAYN FOR-est) A thick forest that receives a large amount of rain during the year.

rosettes (roh-ZETS) The ringlike shapes on the coat of a leopard or jaguar.

scientists (SY-un-tists) People who study the world.

territory (TER-uh-tor-ee) Land or space that an animal guards for its use.

wrestle (REH-sul) To struggle or fight with.

Index

Web Sites

Due to the changing nature of Internet links, PowerKids Press has developed an online list of Web sites related to this book. This site is updated regularly. Please use this link to access the list:

www.powerkidslinks.com/dcats/jaguars/